D1458308

Go, go, go!

First published in 2009
by Wayland

This paperback edition published in 2010 by Wayland

Text copyright © Claire Llewellyn
Illustration copyright © Lauren Beard

Wayland
338 Euston Road
London NW1 3BH

Wayland Australia
Level 17/207 Kent Street
Sydney, NSW 2000

Series Editor: Louise John
Editor: Katie Powell
Cover design: Paul Cherrill
Design: D.R.ink
Consultant: Shirley Bickler

A CIP catalogue record for this book is available from the British Library.

ISBN 9780750259170 (hbk)
ISBN 9780750259354 (pbk)

Printed in China

Wayland is a division of Hachette Children's Books,
an Hachette UK Company

www.hachette.co.uk

Go, go, go!

Written by Claire Llewellyn
Illustrated by Lauren Beard

WAYLAND

We put the buckets
in the car.

We put the spades
in the car.

We put the swimsuits
in the car.

9

We put the towels
in the car.

We put the nets
in the car.

We put the balls
in the car.

We put the drinks
in the car.

We put the sandwiches in the car.

19

Guiding a First Read
Go, go, go!

It is important to talk through the book with the child before they read it alone. This prepares them for the way the story unfolds, and allows them to enjoy the pictures as you both talk naturally, using the language they will later encounter when reading. Read them the brief overview, and then follow the suggestions below:

The high frequency words in this title are:
the   we   in   go

1. Talking through the book

The family is getting ready to go to the beach.
They tell us what they put in the car.

Let's read the title: Go, go, go!
Turn to page 4. Let's have a look at the pictures.
What did they put in the car first?
Yes, they said, "We put the buckets in the car."

Now turn to page 6. What did they say on this page?

Continue to read the book, with the child looking at the illustrations.

2. A first reading of the book

Ask the child to read the book independently and point carefully underneath each word (tracking), while thinking about the story.

Work with the child, prompting them and praising their careful tracking, attempts to correct themselves and their knowledge of letters and sounds:

> **Well done! You saw nets in the picture and the word starts with n. You said 'they' and then changed it to 'we'. Good checking.**

3. Follow-up activities

- Select a high frequency word, as listed on p22, and ask the child to find it throughout the book. Discuss the shape of the letters and the letter sounds.

- To memorise the word, ask the child to write it in the air, then write it repeatedly on a whiteboard or on paper, leaving a space between each attempt.

- Alternate writing the new word starting with a capital letter, and then with a lower-case letter.

4. Encourage

- Rereading of the book many times.

- Drawing a picture based on the story.

- Writing a sentence using the practised word.

START READING is a series of highly enjoyable books for beginner readers. **The books have been carefully graded to match the Book Bands widely used in schools.** This enables readers to be sure they choose books that match their own reading ability.

Look out for the Band colour on the book in our Start Reading logo.

The Bands are:

Pink Band 1A and 1B

Red Band 2

Yellow Band 3

Blue Band 4

Green Band 5

Orange Band 6

Turquoise Band 7

Purple Band 8

Gold Band 9

START READING books can be read independently or shared with an adult. They promote the enjoyment of reading through satisfying stories supported by fun illustrations.

Claire Llewellyn has written many books for children. Some of them are about real things like animals and the Moon, others are storybooks. Claire has two children, but they are getting too big for stories like this one. She hopes you will enjoy reading her stories instead.

Lauren Beard was born in Bolton in 1984. She graduated from Loughborough University in 2006. That same year she came runner up in the Macmillan children's book prize. Since graduating she has had numerous books published and now works in a studio in Manchester.